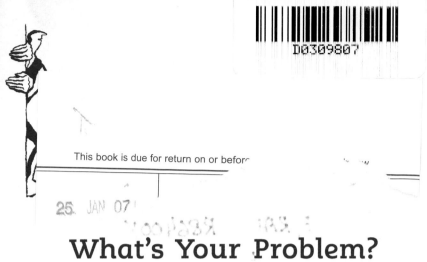

What's Your Problem?

by

Bali Rai

First published in 2003 in Great Britain by
Barrington Stoke Ltd, Sandeman House, Trunk's Close,
55 High Street, Edinburgh EH1 1SR

Reprinted 2004

ISBN 1-842991-26-4

Printed in Great Britain by Bell & Bain Ltd

A Note from the Author

This story is about racism in England. We live in a society where our Government tells us that the extremes of racism are over. The reality is very different.

Every week, in local papers up and down the country, there are reports of racial attacks. Go into any mainly white pub as a member of an ethnic minority (even in your England shirt) and you'll hear abuse. Listen to the racist chanting on the terraces of many football clubs.

I believe that we are ignoring racism because many of us believe that it no longer happens. And when it does, it's always the British National Party or the National Front who are behind it. That just isn't true. There is daily racism from ordinary British people everywhere, most of all in areas with small or non-existent ethnic populations. Racial attacks are increasing as our media and politicians return to the anti–immigrant politics of the past. It often feels as though things are as bad now as they have ever been.

Racism is something that I have fought against most of my life. It is an issue which I feel deserves more attention and that's why I wrote this story. It *is* gritty and it *is*, in places, challenging. There are no quick fixes. But life isn't always easy, most of all if you happen to be an Asian shopkeeper in a mainly white area ...

This story is dedicated to the memory of Stephen Lawrence, and to his family. Ten years since he died, but never forgotten.

To Satpal Ram, now free, after spending years in jail defending his own life against racist thugs.

And to every other victim of racial injustice who I haven't mentioned. Sadly there are too many to list ...

Contents

Chapter 1
A New Start?

My dad scrubbed the window of our newsagent's shop with a mixture of hot water and bleach. The graffiti sprayed on it began to drip down the glass and the letters mingled into each other. The words became unreadable.

The words had said: *Paki Scum Go Home!*

We'd been in this village near Nottingham for two months by then. Moved there from our nice house and our nice lives in good old Leicester. Moved away from our friends.

Moved straight into hell. At least that's what I called it.

We were the only Asian family for miles around. The only brown people that had ever bothered to come to the village. Ever dared to. My dad had called our move a 'new beginning' and a 'new adventure'.

"Never mind what they say about the place," he'd told me and Mum.

"It's got a bad reputation," my mum had replied.

"Oh – what's your problem?" Dad asked her, trying to sound casual. "Just because there are no Indians there – don't mean we'll be getting the grief. Not all white people are racist."

"But ..." I began.

"But nothing, Jaspal. We not letting dirty racists telling us where we can go to or not. Free country, innit."

2

"What about my friends? What about school?"

My dad said nothing.

"What about me?"

I was 14 when my dad sold our first shop and bought the newsagent's. I had been happy in Leicester. I had a school I liked and I had friends. I had a life. Now I was being picked on at my new school. Spat at and called names. And no-one cared. Not my dad. Not my mum. And most of all, not my school teachers. My dad told me that the other kids would get used to me and start to like me. I just had to 'settle in'. "I don't know what your problem is," he'd tell me.

But I didn't want them to get *used* to me. I didn't want to have to *settle in*. It made me sound like I was a freak of some kind. An alien child landed from the Planet Weirdo, who had yet to learn the ways and customs of his new home. Sod that. I wasn't an alien.

The only difference between me and the other kids was that I was brown and English and they were white and English.

I spoke the same way as they did. I liked the same bands and computer games. I mostly ate the same food too – burgers, chips, pizzas and all that. And I bet they all ate curry.

Sometimes I wished I really was an alien from the Planet Weirdo. At least then I could hope to fly off into space to be with people who liked me for the person I was. I didn't want to stay in the village, trying to avoid all the ignorant scumbags who only saw my colour.

I wanted to be somewhere where I could get away from the daily racial abuse and bullying. A place where my parents weren't afraid for their lives after dark. A place where my dad didn't have to wash racist graffiti off the shop window. And my mum didn't have to clean up the dog shit posted through the letterbox. Somewhere like our old home.

****

During our first week in the village our newsagent's shop stayed closed. My dad was working there – adding extra shelf space and changing the layout so that he would sell more.

One or two of the locals had popped their heads around the door to say hello. There was Mr Wright from the off-licence next door and Mrs Filbert, who owned the flower shop over the road. They were both normal. Nice, even.

"Ey oop, m'duck!" Mrs Filbert had said when I'd been outside the shop one day.

"Hello," I had said.

"Is it your dad what's openin' the paper shop?" she'd asked.

"Yeah – we've just moved out here from Leicester."

"I'll have to pop in for a cuppa tea then," she'd said, smiling.

Mr Wright had walked in as my dad was sorting out the new electronic till – the old one had been an antique.

"Ey oop, Mr Sangha," he'd said. He'd already met my dad when my parents had come to look at the place.

"Mornin' Mr Wright – how things?" my dad had answered.

"Call me Jimmy will yer," Mr Wright said.

"And you calling me Satnam," replied my dad, smiling.

Everything was all right up to that point.

The shop opened on the Saturday morning before I was due to start at my new school. My mum and dad smiled to each other as I went out and put the 'open' sign outside on the pavement. I went back in, grabbed a computer magazine from the shelves and ducked behind the counter. I settled on a stool next to my dad and we waited for the first customer to come in.

Five minutes later a group of three young boys walked in. They looked about ten or eleven. One of them came up to the counter. He had greasy red hair and freckles.

"Ten B&H, mate," he said. My dad looked at him, smiled and shook his head.

"Sorry son, no fags. You under the age," he said.

The boy smirked and turned to his friends.

"'Ee won't give me no fags," he told them.

The other two walked up to the counter. One of them picked up a bar of chocolate. He opened it, took a big bite and put the rest back.

"Forty-nine pence, please," I said to him. My dad stood up.

"I don't wan' it," the boy told me.

"I don't care," said my dad. "You eat it so you got to pay, innit."

The boys looked at each other and started laughing. The red-haired one made a nasty sound in his throat and then spat something green and slimy onto the counter. I went mad. I shot up from my stool and made for the other side of the counter. My dad grabbed me by the arm.

"Leave it, Jaspal," he told me, in Punjabi.

Leave it? How could I leave it?

My dad stayed calm and told the boys to get out. One of them asked us which part of Afghanistan we were from. Then the red-haired one yelled, "*Pakis!*" at us and they ran out of the shop. I wanted to go after them but my dad just went into the back for a cloth and then cleaned up their mess. As he wiped the spit from the counter, our neighbour, Mr Wright, came in.

"Them little scumbags giving you trouble, Satnam?" he asked. He was bald on top and rather plump. When he spoke his voice creaked and his face went all red.

"No problem, Jimmy. Usual kids messin' 'bout an' that," my dad told him.

"They were being racist," I said, not wanting to hide the truth from Mr Wright.

"Ah – they've no brains – that's all," Mr Wright told me. "That age – they don't know what racism is. They just think it's clever."

I was about to say something in reply but my dad told me to get something from the flat above the shop. I was about to argue but he had this look on his face. The kind of look that told me he wasn't in the mood for games. I did what he said.

The rest of that first day passed without any problems and on the Sunday everything was fine until my dad closed up the shop at just after five in the afternoon. I was restocking the shelves when a letter was pushed under the door. I looked up to see two people running away. I went to the window but they had gone by the time I got there. My dad was in the stockroom so I picked up the envelope and took it to him.

"What's that?" he asked me.

"Dunno," I shrugged, handing it to him. "Someone just pushed it under the door."

He opened the letter and his face went grim as he read it. I asked him what was up but he said nothing. He screwed the letter up and threw it to the floor. I wanted to know. I picked up the letter and opened it out. At the top was a logo. It was a fist. A white fist on a green Nazi swastika. My stomach turned over. I read the letter. It was typed:

To our recently arrived friends,

We, The Brotherhood Of The White Fist, would like you to understand the following:

We will never allow this village to be contaminated by filth like you. Get out now and no harm will come to you. Ignore us and you will be made to pay the price. You stick to your cities and we'll stick to our towns and villages.

You have been warned,

The Brotherhood Of The White Fist. Fighting for a pure nation.

I looked at my dad. I was angry and scared at the same time.

"I knew we shouldn't have come here," I told him.

"Don't worry, Jaspal – it's only kids messing."

"It don't sound like they are messing about to me," I replied. "We should call the police."

"No – no police. They just have to getting used to us," my dad said. He was looking defiant.

"Dad, that letter is a threat," I pointed out.

"Soon getting better," he said. "This happen every time Indian opening business in white area."

I shook my head at him. *Soon get better?* I had to go to school the next day and I wasn't looking forward to that.

Chapter 2
School

It was sunny and warm the following morning, as I waited for the school bus. There was a special service that took the pupils from our village to the school in a nearby town.

Although the sun was warm and the sky was blue, I was feeling less than happy. The threatening letter was on my mind and I was worried about what was going to happen when I got to my new school. Two younger kids were also waiting for the bus. They ignored me. They were busy arguing over a computer game that one of them had 'borrowed' from the other and forgotten to give back.

Across the road my dad had already been open for two hours. I could see him through the window, checking stock and moving things around. Every now and then people walked in and bought newspapers and cigarettes and stuff.

I didn't want to go to school. I wanted to help Dad out instead. Make sure that he didn't get any more grief from the locals. And I didn't want to be reminded of my old school and my old friends. I knew that as soon as I stepped into my new school, memories of my old life would come flooding back into my head and make me feel even more homesick.

At last, the bus pulled up and the doors whined open. I let the other two get on first, hoping there would still be empty seats. But they were nearly all full. As I climbed aboard, I felt that everyone was staring at me, like I had two heads or something.

I turned and looked down the bus. Most people were now looking down or out of the window. Some of the pupils started to chat again, but a gang of lads at the back just sat and stared at me. I looked for a spare seat and saw one, halfway down the bus, beside a girl with red hair and glasses. I walked towards her and asked her if the seat was free. She looked at me and smiled. I felt a bit better. I sat down and thanked the girl.

"No prob," she smiled, "I'm Katie."

"Hi, I'm Jas," I replied, smiling back, and thinking that she had a very pretty smile.

Behind us I heard some of the boys snigger and then someone coughed and mumbled something under his breath.

"Sorry, Cutler – what was that you were sayin'?" a clearer voice added.

"It's a shame that them effing Pakis can't stay in their own country," the boy called Cutler said much louder.

"Oh right. I thought you were saying there were too many *Pakis* on this bus."

The hairs on the back of my neck stood up and my legs felt like all the blood had left them. I started to clench and unclench my fists. The girl sitting next to me, Katie, put her hand on my leg.

"Take no notice," she whispered. "They're just trying to wind you up."

I didn't say a word, but I was fuming. The lads at the back just went on sniggering.

"Hey, Steggsy – maybe we could help send 'em back 'ome," said another voice. So it went on all the way to school. As they stormed off the bus, the biggest one came up to me.

"A'right, darkie?" he said, sneering at me. "I'm Steggsy – we'll be seein' a lot of each other ..."

And he left the bus. I was so angry that I didn't want to get off the bus. I just sat there, staring out of the window. In the end the bus driver came up and told me that I had to get off. I just looked at him.

"Did you hear what they called me?" I asked him.

The driver shook his head.

"Sorry, son. I didn't hear a thing. Can't hear nothin' up at front of the bus."

"You must have – everyone else did."

"Well they were probably just teasin' yer," he said. I looked away and then back at him, my cheeks burning with rage.

"It was racial abuse," I told him. "That's against the law."

17

"Listen, son, I didn't hear a thing. I dunno what your problem is. If you're going to come to our country you should get used to our sense of humour ..."

And then he pointed at the door.

"Now, son, if yer don't mind I've got to go and pick up some more kids."

I got up and barged past him, swearing at him under my breath. I stepped off the bus and looked around. My new school. I thought about my old one, in Leicester, with its concrete tennis courts and the high-rise blocks towering behind it. There had been the constant noise of traffic and sirens and people shouting at each other. And then I listened to the birdsong and shook my head.

"Man, what a dump," I said to no-one in particular.

Five minutes later I was sitting by the reception desk in the entrance hall when I saw Katie and another girl. She was blonde and she was smiling at me. I looked away, feeling a bit embarrassed. The blonde girl was really pretty and she was looking right at me. She walked over and stuck out her hand.

"Hiya! I'm Jemma," she said with a big smile.

I stood up and shook her hand.

"Er ... hi. I'm Jas."

"You've already met Katie. Come on. We're here to take you to your new class."

We walked up three flights of stairs and down a corridor to the far end. At the very last room, Jemma stopped and smiled at me again. Katie had said nothing during the short walk.

"This is C16 – our form room," she said.

"We're in the same form?" I asked.

"Yeah!" she said. "There's four forms in each year and we're the best!"

"Oh," I said, because I couldn't think of anything else to say.

"Come on," added Katie, opening the door. "Come and meet everyone."

We stepped in and I counted 20 pupils, including myself. The teacher, a young man with spiky hair and an earring, was calling out the register. Once he had finished he told the rest of the class to wait while he talked to me.

"Hello, Jaspal," he said, "I'm Mr Kitson – I'll be your tutor for the next two years."

I smiled at him.

"Hi – and call me Jas," I told him.

"No prob – Jas. Did you get here all right?"

"Yeah," I lied, not wanting to break my old school rule of never grassing anyone up.

"Good, good. Let's introduce you to everyone else."

So Kitson introduced me. I looked around at the faces in front of me and for the first time it hit me how different I was from them. There wasn't a single non-white face in there. Just me. Kitson told me all their names and then showed me to an empty place.

I was sitting between Katie and Jemma. I noticed that some of the others were staring at me and whispering. It was 'new kid' gossip – I'd done it often enough myself at my old school. For now I was the centre of attention.

"Right!" said Kitson, after a few minutes. "Jemma, Katie and Jas stay here with me and the rest of you get going."

Someone wolf-whistled and the class started laughing.

"Yeah, yeah," said Kitson, dismissing them. "Those of you I should be taking for English first period will have the pleasure of Mrs Parker-Brown's company for today."

A groan went up.

"Mrs Parker-Brown's the principal," Jemma whispered to me.

"And I'll see you all after lunch," Kitson went on. "Oh and remember we've got our GCSE meeting this afternoon."

The rest of the kids filed out of the classroom. Most of them stopped to take another good look at me. Some smiled. When they'd gone, Kitson smiled at me and told me I would be shown around the school and get to know the rules. My pupil 'buddies' would be Katie and Jemma. I was secretly quite pleased about that. They seemed nice.

"OK," said Kitson, making a real effort to be nice. "Let's start with the timetable ..."

Chapter 3

Steggsy

I spent the morning learning the school rules and finding out where everything was. My timetable was easy to understand and it seemed to be the same as Katie's and Jemma's. I spent the lunch hour with Katie in the classroom, filling out forms and getting ready for school life.

"You didn't tell Kitson about what happened this morning, did you?" she asked me as I ate a sandwich.

"Don't matter," I told her.

"Those lads on the bus are thick anyway," she said. "Year Eleven wasters."

"Who's the big one – the one that spoke to me when he was getting off the bus?"

Katie gave me a funny look.

"Steggsy?" she asked.

"Yeah, him."

"He's an idiot. Hardly ever comes to school and even when he does he causes trouble."

"Oh," I said.

"His real name is Jason," she said.

"So why Steggsy?"

"Steggles," she replied. "Jason Steggles."

I pretended not to care, even though just thinking about him made me angry.

"He's Jemma's stepbrother," said Katie.

"Really?"

"Yeah – she hates him. But don't worry.
He won't last until the end of the year.
I reckon he'll be gone by Christmas."

"Why do you think that?" I asked.

Katie smiled, just as Jemma walked into
the room.

"Because he'll get into trouble. He always
does," she said. Jemma looked at us both and
asked who we were talking about.

"Your darling stepbrother," Katie told her.

"Why? What's he done now?"

I looked out of the window as Katie told
Jemma about the bus incident.

"Wait till I see him ..." replied Jemma
angrily.

"Please don't say anything," I told her.
"I can look after myself."

Then Jemma asked me about my old school. I spent the rest of lunch talking about it, as if to talk about it might somehow bring it closer. Then, as the bell went for afternoon registration, an old lady with grey hair and weird, rimmed glasses came in. It was Mrs Parker-Brown, the principal.

"Good afternoon," she said, in a very slow, very posh voice.

She came over and stood beside me. "You'll like our little school," she told me.

"It's very nice," I replied.

"This school was very popular in the Victorian age," she continued.

"Really?" I said.

"Yes ... many of our pupils went out into the Empire – to help civilise and educate the natives. I'm sure, that being an Indian, that is something you'll appreciate."

I didn't know whether to laugh or cry. She was mad.

"Anyway, just thought I'd introduce myself to you," finished Mrs Parker-Brown.

She walked off without looking back and shut the door behind her very gently.

"Is she off her head?" I said.

Jemma burst out laughing. "She's completely bonkers, the old bag," she said. "She thinks that the country is going to the dogs and that young people are too obsessed with freedom. Most of all women ..."

"I wouldn't mind," I said, "but I ain't even Indian. I was born here."

"Well, what a lovely first day you've had so far," said Katie. "Ignorance and racial abuse. Hmm ... *Would you like that to go?* as they say in McDonald's."

Then Mr Kitson walked in.

27

"I see you've met our principal," he said, smiling in a knowing way. "Now I think it's about time you joined the rest of your class."

So I settled down to wait for the rest of the class and tried to ignore the fact that Jemma was staring at me, even though I was secretly pleased.

I got off the school bus with Katie. I was feeling a little bit better. The afternoon had gone well and I had even quite enjoyed my first maths lesson. I didn't even like maths but it was nice to get a lesson, any lesson, out of the way. I walked Katie back to her house before heading off to my parents'.

The village was quite small and my dad's newsagent's was on the main road. I suppose the village was pretty in its way – lots of little cottages and big old houses with perfect gardens full of brightly coloured flowers. It was a different world to the place I had grown up in. But maybe it would be OK. *Once they've got used to me*, I thought to myself. But then I thought, *Why should I wait for them to get used to me? They should accept me or get lost,* another part of my brain was saying.

As I turned into the main road, I passed a pub and came to a small playground area. I didn't notice Steggsy and his crew until they were behind me. I felt a kick on the back of my leg and span round to see Steggsy and three other lads standing there smirking. I clenched my fists, my heart pumping.

"I told you you'd be seein' a lot of me," sneered Steggsy.

"*And?*" I stood my ground and stared him out, using everything I'd learned growing up in inner city Leicester. You never let a bully know you're scared of him. Never.

The other lads sniggered, hiding behind their leader. One of them, a greasy, rat-faced lad, egged his mate on.

"Go on, Steggsy, batter him!"

Steggsy looked at me and then spat on the ground.

"You ain't welcome round here, *Paki*," he said, trying to get me to react, but I just held his gaze.

"You listenin' to me?" he asked.

I turned and started to walk away, scared but angry too. That was when they jumped me. I felt a punch to the back of my head and then my legs were swept from underneath me. I could hear them calling me racist names and as I tried to get up, I swung out a fist and it connected with a face. The lad I hit started crying.

I got up and threw another punch, this one at Steggsy. It caught him in the mouth and his lip split. He squealed like a girl and kicked me. Then the rest of them jumped in, punching and kicking.

At last someone came out of the pub and chased them off. By this point I was on the floor, my nose and mouth bleeding and a pain around my left eye.

"You all right, son?" asked a man standing above me.

He helped me up and I dusted myself down, picking up my bag.

"Yeah," I told him, "it was nothing ..."

"Do you want me to call the police?"

I thought about it but decided it would only cause me more trouble if I grassed Steggsy up.

"No thanks, mate," I said. "Thanks all the same."

The man gave me a strange look, like I was stupid, and then shrugged.

"You take care then," he said. "I'll probably see you in your dad's newsagent's."

I thanked him again and walked home slowly. As I walked in my mum gasped and made me sit down, calling my dad.

"What happened?" he asked in Punjabi.

"Nothing, Dad – just some bullies at school."

"We should call your teacher," said my mum.

"Nah ... I'll be fine. It's nothing."

"But, *beteh*, you are bleeding," she went on.

I looked up at my dad and there were tears welling in my eyes.

"What did you expect?" I shouted. "Bringing me to this dump of a village ..."

"But, *beteh* ..."

"NO! It's your fault. YOURS!" I screamed at him.

With that, I acted like a spoilt kid and ran to my room. I didn't come out again until much later. I felt guilty that I'd shouted at my dad and stupid for acting like an eight year old ...

Chapter 4
The Warning

The next day I got on the bus and found a seat next to Jemma and Katie. I looked towards the back where Steggsy and his crew always sat. He wasn't there but two of the other lads were, the skinny, rat-faced one called Chas, and the fat, blonde one, Cutler.

I stared at them, expecting some abuse, but they looked at anything but me. Down at the floor, out the window. Just not at me. *Typical*, I thought, as I sat down, *no balls when their leader wasn't around.*

Katie and Jemma started asking me about my black eye and the cuts on my face.

"It's nothing," I told them, looking away.

"Nothing?" said Jemma, frowning, "You look like you've run into a wall or something."

"Who was it, Jas?" asked Katie.

"It wasn't anyone ... just some trouble. Nothing I can't handle. I'll deal with it my way," I told them.

Katie and Jemma looked at me with a mixture of pity and concern. I went red and looked out of the window, wishing that they would leave it alone.

I spent the morning of my second day at my new school unable to concentrate on a word the teachers were saying. My mind was on Steggsy and his mates and how I was going to deal with them the next time they came for me. It wasn't a question of *whether* they would come. More of *when*. I was thankful when the bell went for lunchtime.

After lunch I sat in a dream through biology and history. I wanted to get home to my bedroom where I could lock the door and put on my headphones and listen to my music.

Jemma picked up on my mood on the way home and kept asking me what was up. I was grateful for her interest but I didn't tell her about the attack.

But I could think of nothing else. I felt ashamed that I hadn't put up a better fight. That I had felt scared. That wasn't how I'd been brought up. That wasn't what I'd learned in Leicester, where an attack like that would have been dealt with the same night. Only in Leicester I'd have had back-up. Here in the perfect English village I had just me.

When I got in I put some hip-hop on and turned up the volume, getting lost in each track, but still not forgetting what was on my mind. I didn't even hear my mum knocking on my door until she just about broke it down. Taking off my headphones, I jumped off my bed and unlocked the door.

"Are you deaf, Jaspal?" she shouted, in Punjabi.

"Sorry, Mum, I was listening to some music," I replied in English.

"Go downstairs and help your father."

"Why?" I asked. I didn't think the shop was all that busy.

"He is doing some paperwork so he needs you to mind the counter," replied my mum.

"Cool."

I turned off my stereo and headed downstairs and out into the shop.

"You watching counter, *beteh*," said my dad in English.

"OK."

"I'll be in back doing papers ..."

"No problem, Dad. I ain't got no homework anyway," I replied.

He shuffled off into the back with a big red file full of his order sheets and stuff.

I settled down on the stool and waited for a customer, watching the small telly that my dad had under the counter. Every two or three minutes people came in and bought the evening paper or fags. Most of them were polite but one or two made comments under their breath, mainly stuff I couldn't understand because they had mumbled it. I ignored it all and waited for my dad to finish what he was doing.

It was nearly an hour later when two men came in, sneering at me and then smiling to each other. I sensed trouble straight away. There was just something in the way that they were looking at me. And each other. The taller of the two was shaven-headed and wearing a Nottingham Forest shirt with combat trousers and boots. A spider's web tattoo crawled up the right side of his thick neck and he had a bulldog wrapped in the Union Jack on his left arm with the letters *BWF* underneath it.

The other man was shorter than me but twice as wide and had a five-inch-long scar running down the left side of his face. He was wearing a combat jacket, jeans and boots, and he too was close-shaven. He was the sort of racist thug that you meet in your nightmares. One of the 'NFs' my dad always told me about. National Front. Racist scum.

As if to confirm this, he pulled up his jacket sleeves. On one arm he had a tattoo of a Union Jack with *NF* in the middle of the red cross and *England's Pride* written above and below. On the other arm was a naked lady. A dagger dripped blood between her breasts. I caught myself staring and looked away quickly. The shorter man spoke first.

"Twenny B&H." Just like that. No please. No mate.

I coughed. My dad must have realised that I was trying to catch his attention, because he walked in and looked at the two men. He told me to sit down, in Punjabi, and faced the shorter man.

"What you after, mate?" he asked, smiling.

"What's your problem – can't you speak?" said the shorter man, in a deep growl of a voice, looking at me and ignoring my dad.

"He busy – I serving. What you want?" my dad asked.

The taller man sneered and leaned into my dad's face.

"You know what we want," he said. "And don't call him 'mate' – he ain't no mate of yours."

The shorter man smiled and showed two gold teeth.

"Twenny B&H," he spat out.

My dad turned and got the fags from the shelf and put them down on the counter. He waited for the money. The taller man looked around and then pulled a 20 pound note from his trousers, screwed it up and threw it into my dad's face. I got angry and stood up but the man just laughed at me and then his face got deadly serious.

"Sit down, Paki," he whispered to me. "I'm not here to hurt yer unless you make me."

I stood my ground and stared into his pale blue eyes. They didn't blink once.

"Leicester's easy to go back to," he told my dad.

"You can just jump in yer Paki wagon and 40 minutes from now you'll be back in Pakistan," added the short one.

My dad told them the price of the fags and waited. I could tell that he was fuming, but he didn't show it.

"Just a friendly piece of advice," said the taller man. He picked up the 20 from the counter where it had fallen and smoothed it before putting it back on the counter.

My dad picked it up and cashed up the fags, laying the change down on the counter. The shorter man picked up the money and pocketed it while the other one started to sniff the air.

"Smell that?" he whispered, to no-one in particular. "Smells like petrol."

He looked me in the eye and smiled.

"Just like petrol," he repeated before both of them left the shop.

My dad went around to the front of the counter after the two men and locked the door behind them. He turned to me and tried to smile. Tried to pretend it was nothing.

"They just idiots, innit," he said, not looking me in the eye.

"I think you should report them to the coppers," I said, trying to stay calm.

"No point, *beteh*. They not doing anything. Just messing 'bout," replied my dad, not looking at all sure about what he was saying.

"Dad – they weren't messing about. At least report them – that way ..."

"No, Jaspal. I don't care about them mens. It's my country too."

I shook my head and went back upstairs, wondering when the next warning would come.

Chapter 5

The Second Letter

For the next couple of months things went on pretty much the same way. I got more involved at school and spent lots of time with Jemma and Katie and another couple of lads, John and Sam, who I played football with for the school team. Katie fancied Sam. She went bright red every time she saw him.

I began to settle into school but the racism didn't stop and part of me never gave up hope of moving back to Leicester. But my dad just accepted it all and got on with running the shop, ignoring all the abuse. On more than one occasion groups of youths would come in and throw stuff on the floor or push over a display, calling us asylum seekers and illegal immigrants and much stronger stuff.

One lad came in every day to get his dad's papers, and he always asked my dad what it was like leaving Afghanistan to come to England. No matter how many times my dad told the little idiot that we were English Punjabis, he still carried on.

In the end, my dad banned him from the shop and he sent his old man in. The kid's dad told my dad that he would have a word with his son but thought that it was a bit rich for us to come to *their* village and start banning people from *their* newsagent's.

Typical ignorant rubbish.

Two serious things happened around that time. One night my dad went outside to bring in the shop sign and a car full of white lads drove by really slowly, like they had been waiting for him to come out. They threw a full can of beer at his head. It caught him above his right eyebrow and knocked him to the ground. The blood was running into his eye. But even when Mr Wright from the shop next door told him to call the police, my dad just shrugged it off and told him that they weren't going to run him out of the village.

I had to take over the shop the next day and missed a day at school, because my dad felt sick from the knock he took to the head.

Two nights after my dad was attacked, my mum was crossing the road when another car full of lads tried to run her over. She had gone over to Mrs Filbert's shop to give her some samosas and was coming back when she heard tyres screeching. She'd looked up to see a car hurtling towards her and had dived forward, tearing her clothing and grazing her hands, arms and face. She'd walked into the shop crying. I went mad and ran out into the street, looking for someone, anyone, to hit.

But the street was empty. In the end I came back inside and called the police myself, telling my dad that enough was enough. My dad didn't even reply – he just stood where he was, looking at my mum, not saying a word, like he was in shock.

The police took half an hour to arrive and from the start they looked as though they couldn't have cared less. One of them took a statement from my mum, which I had to translate, and the other one spoke to my dad. They did what they had to and then told us that they would send along a hate-crimes officer to see us. And they left – just like that.

I asked my mum if she wanted to go to the hospital. She told me that she'd be OK and went to bed. She didn't say anything to my dad.

I closed up the shop and found my dad in the living room, staring at the telly with a glass of whisky in his hands. He stayed up the whole night and in the morning I had to run the shop again.

Things were tense for a few days after that. The hate-crimes officer turned up. She spoke to my mum through me and then she spoke to my dad. She told us that what had happened was terrible and then left us a number to call if anything else happened.

Two hours later someone pushed an envelope full of dog shit through the letterbox and I had to clean the mess up. I was so angry I had tears in my eyes and if I had had a gun – well, I'd have ended up in prison that night.

The abuse continued – everyday – at school from Steggsy and his crew or in the shop from kids, adults, even pensioners.

It was like a bad dream. I stopped sleeping properly and my school work began to suffer. My dad was drinking too much and

my mum refused to go out without me or my
dad to protect her. It was October now and
dark by the time I got home from school,
often just escaping a run-in with Steggsy.
That was all I could think about.

The only good part was the time I spent
with my new friends, most of all Jemma who
was really keen on me. In the end she asked
me if I wanted to go on a date with her, to
the cinema in Nottingham, and I said yes.
The film was really good and it was nice to be
in a city with normal people who even looked
like me every now and then. I didn't feel like
an outsider so much. I was almost happy
when we left the cinema for the last bus out
to the village.

But then, on the way home, on the bus,
people were staring at me. Some lads
threatened me and I stopped feeling relaxed.
All the tension came flooding back. We got
off at our stop and I walked Jemma home.
I kissed her goodnight and told her that I'd

see her on the school bus in the morning. I set off for home, staying in the light of the streetlamps where I could, tense and nervous all the way. I was certain that I would get jumped or something. I didn't, but some lads in a passing car shouted insults at me and told me I was dead. My mood wasn't helped by my dad when I got in. He asked me where I'd been and with who.

"I thought you wanted me to make friends here," I said, wanting nothing more than to go to my bedroom.

"You not telling me you were going to be late ..."

"It's not late, Dad. It's only just gone 11."

My dad sighed and told me that he'd been worried about me.

"I told you we should go back to Leicester," I said. *That would stop all the worrying,* I thought.

My dad shook his head.

"How can we hold up our heads knowing that we ran away from these *people*?" he asked in Punjabi.

"Who cares?" I said.

"I do, *beteh*. I do."

"But, Dad, things are just going to get worse – not better."

"No," he said, fiercely. "We are men just like them. We not bloody animals."

"Dad ..."

"Nah, *beteh*. If we run they winning ... you want them to beat you?"

I shook my head at him and told him I was off to bed. He sighed again and poured himself another whisky.

The next morning the second letter arrived. It had the same logo, a green swastika with a white fist. I looked at the typed message:

How many warnings will it take for your sub-human brains to get our message? Go home today or face the consequences.

We will not allow asylum seekers, illegal immigrants and terrorists into our areas. We will fight to defend our country. Take your dirty culture and go back home.

You have been warned once again,

The Brotherhood Of The White Fist. Fighting for a pure nation.

I tore it up and chucked it in the bin. At once I was sorry I'd done that. I had just destroyed important evidence. I fished out the bits of paper, put them in the envelope, stuffed the whole lot into my school bag and headed for the bus stop, without saying anything to my dad. He had enough on his plate already. Things were about to get worse too. Much worse.

Chapter 6

The Fight

It was during November that everything came to a head. Everything that had gone on up to that point had been a build-up to the real thing. Like those computer games where you get an easy level to start off with – before you really get stuffed with the hard bits.

It's hard to admit but you get used to the everyday abuse once it's been happening for long enough. It becomes part of your life. Your routine. It's like getting up in the morning, cleaning your teeth, catching the bus.

I stopped getting so angry over the comments about immigrants. I didn't get mad with the little kids who called my mum a brown slag and spat at her in the street. I stopped wanting to kill everyone that racially abused my dad as they bought their fags and papers and milk.

Thinking about it now, it's quite sad that I *did* get so used to it. But when it's as everyday as watching your favourite soap opera, it becomes normal. Or at least you forget what *normal* is and go with what you get.

The week started like any other. There was another threatening letter, more graffiti on the window and people opening the shop door just to shout abuse.

At school I was still trying to put a brave face on everything. I spent my time with

Jemma and Katie, and kept one eye open for Steggsy and his boys. I'd heard rumours that he'd threatened to 'do me' because I'd been seen with Jemma, his stepsister. That he was going to deal with me once and for all. I ignored it all because he would only bully me when his crew were around and never bothered me on his own.

I was more concerned with the racist group that were sending letters to my dad's shop. Each letter was more threatening than the last. My dad was drinking more and more, stubborn as ever.

But it was my mum who was most affected by it all. She had started to lose weight and couldn't sleep at night. Her hair, which had still been quite dark when we'd left Leicester, was now almost completely grey. She stayed inside, always upstairs, refusing to go out or into the shop. I felt helpless. Useless. There was nothing that I could do and to tell you the truth it was killing me.

Looking back on it, I suppose what I did was due to my feelings at the time and not just a reaction to the abuse. In fact, I *know* that's what made me do what I did ...

****

It was Tuesday and I was sitting in a geography lesson. I was trying to think straight. Sam had overheard two of Steggsy's crew say that they'd be waiting for me after school. The night before I had walked Jemma home and Steggsy had seen us kissing outside her house. He was fuming.

All through the afternoon I had been trying to decide whether it was just another 'I'm gonna get the Paki' rumour or whether Steggsy was really going to have a go at me. After all, everyone knew that I was seeing Jemma and Steggsy had a reputation to keep up. What was he going to do? Just accept that I was seeing his stepsister or try and play the hard man?

I didn't know then that he was a Brotherhood member – I found that out later – I just knew that he would have to do something to stop his mates from thinking he was soft.

When the bell went I picked up my bag and followed the rest of my class out of school, keeping an eye out for Steggsy. There were loads of kids waiting by the bus stop and I hung back a bit, waiting to see Jemma and Katie. I noticed that there was a group of about 30 pupils waiting around and looking at me. Sam was one of them and he came over.

"You better get home, Jas," he said to me. "Steggsy is coming for you."

I looked up at Sam.

"I don't care, Sam," I told him, hoping that Steggsy would hurry up so that we could get it over with. I wasn't scared but I wouldn't say that I felt confident either. I just saw it as yet another bit of hassle.

"Jas – just go home. It ain't worth it," replied Sam, trying to get me to see sense.

"He'll only do the same thing tomorrow," I said.

"So we'll tell Kitson or something ..."

"Nah – you go home if you like, mate. I'm not running from no-one."

I thought about how much I sounded like my dad, stubborn and proud. The crowd grew bigger. It continued to grow for about five minutes and then all of a sudden it parted. Steggsy and his crew came walking over, grim smiles on their faces. I stood up and pushed Sam to one side.

"You'd better go, Sam," I told him. "This is my fight."

Sam didn't move. Instead, he put down his bag and clenched his fists. I could hear the crowd beginning to murmur in excitement. There was going to be a fight.

Steggsy stopped about two metres away from where I stood.

"Leave my sister alone," he said.

"Piss off."

I couldn't think of anything else to say.

"You don't get it, do yer?" said Steggsy. "Leave my sister alone, you darkie – or I'm gonna do you and yer parents."

I got angry at the mention of my mum and dad.

"I thought you were a hard man?" I said, hoping to embarrass him. "But all you're doin' is talking ..."

I clenched my fists, ready for punches and kicks to come raining down on me but they didn't. At least not at once. Steggsy rolled up his sleeve and flexed his arm. There was a new tattoo on it, a bulldog wrapped in the

Union Jack with the letters *BWF* underneath it. I had seen it before.

"You just don't get it, do yer?" shouted Steggsy. "This is bigger than the playground ... stick to yer own kind or we'll be paying yer a visit." He flexed his new tattoo again.

I looked at the other lads and then back at Steggsy. I shrugged my shoulders.

"I'm sick of all this," I told them. "You wanna fight – let's go."

The punches came in from Steggsy, one after the other, with no power behind them. I protected my head and then took a step back to steady myself, standing like a boxer, right hand tucked in and left ready to jab – just like I'd learnt at kickboxing. Steggsy was fighting like a football hooligan – just throwing out punches and kicks – so I let him wear himself down. He caught me a few times, but even though the blows hurt I didn't run.

I waited and waited and then kicked him in his groin. As he went down on one knee, holding himself, I punched him twice with my left fist to the side of his head and then drove my right fist under his chin. The impact made me cry out in pain and Steggsy's head rocked back like it was on a length of elastic.

He tried to get up but I was in a rage by then. All I could think about was my mum and dad and all the abuse that we had taken. I hit him again, in the same place, and then kicked him in the rib cage. That was it. Sam jumped on me and dragged me away. I could hear the crowd, saw the other lads run off and then I looked at Steggsy. He was on his back, his head in a puddle, out cold.

I shrugged off Sam and got my bag, pulling out the second letter from the Brotherhood, the one that I had torn up and then fished out of the bin. I looked down at Steggsy, swore at him and then emptied the contents of the envelope over him. Then, calm as anything, I walked through the onlookers, and out into the street.

I didn't talk to anyone all the way home and when I got in I ignored my mobile and told my mum that if anyone rang – *anyone* – that I wasn't at home. And then I locked myself in my room and turned on some music.

It was half past nine when I went downstairs. My mobile was ringing. It was Jemma.

"Are you upset with me about Steggsy?" I asked.

"I'm upset that you had to fight him when you could have just told Kitson or someone."

"Yeah – I'm sorry. It won't happen again."

She didn't say anything for a moment.

"Look, we'll talk tomorrow," she said in the end.

"Yeah – is he OK?"

"Who?"

"Steggsy."

"I don't know – he's at his dad's – my mum and him have split up again."

"Oh …"

This time I was silent for a moment.

"I'll see you on the bus," Jemma told me.

"OK."

I pushed the red end-call button and threw the phone onto my bed. I wondered what Steggsy would do. Whether his threats were real. I didn't want to be fighting in the streets like some animal. I didn't want to have to worry all the time about what was going to happen around the next corner or down the next street.

I just wanted to be accepted for who I was. I remember being so angry with everything and everyone. And even with myself. I didn't have long to wait to find out what Steggsy would do next either. It all kicked off big time the next day.

Chapter 7

Suspended

It had been Mrs Parker-Brown, the principal, who had found Steggsy lying in the puddle.

She had called an ambulance and the police straight away.

She had tried to find out what had happened from a bunch of Year Nines. Some of them had told her that there had been a fight, but Steggsy, when he had come round, had refused to say who had beaten him up or why. The police had left it at that, and

Steggsy had gone home after the ambulance men had checked him over.

The following morning, Mrs Parker-Brown found a note under her door telling her it was me. She had no idea who the note was from, but I could have guessed for her. It had to be Steggsy's crew. Cutler probably. Either way, as soon as registration was over, Kitson told me to remain behind and told me everything.

"Why, Jas?" he'd asked me.

I just shrugged.

"It doesn't seem like the kind of thing that you'd do," he said, playing with some folders on his desk.

"How do you know?" I replied, not looking at him.

"Because ..."

"Because I've been here for three months and you think you know me?"

"I feel I'm getting to know you," he sighed.

"It's nothing," I said, "just one of those playground things."

"Only it's not," he told me, looking all serious.

"Why?"

"Because Jason Steggles was found lying in a puddle by the principal of the school, that's why. Because this kind of thing isn't tolerated at this school. Because Mrs Parker-Brown is going to suspend you until it's all sorted out."

I looked out of the window and shrugged again, trying to pretend that I couldn't care less. But inside I was shocked. And angry.

"He was bullying me," I said, after a while.

"Bullying *you*? He's obviously not a good bully," smiled Kitson, trying to lighten the situation. It didn't work.

"Racist stuff – ever since I got here."

"Why didn't you report it?"

"For *what*? Ain't like you can do anything about it."

"Yes we can – the school has a clear policy on racism and bullying."

"What – you gonna get them to change their *minds*? Change their *views*?"

Kitson looked at me and then sighed.

"No – but we can make them see that it's not acceptable in this school."

"What about outside the gates – back in the village?"

"Is this something that goes beyond the school?" asked Kitson.

"Never mind – how long am I suspended for?"

Kitson looked out of the window this time. He waited for a few moments before he spoke again.

"One week and then you'll have to go and explain yourself to the school governors. You and Jason Steggles."

"So I'm suspended as of now?" I asked.

"Yes – but you have to go and see Mrs Parker-Brown before you go home."

I shrugged again and looked out at the trees and the fields beyond the school.

I wondered what my dad would do. It wasn't the first time I'd been suspended but at least this time it wasn't my fault. I mean what was I supposed to do – just let Steggsy carry on bullying me?

"Right – get yourself over to Mrs Parker-Brown's office," said Kitson.

I got up and grabbed my bag.

"And, Jas – next time speak to me. If there's more to this than just bullying at school, then I need to know. I can help."

"What you going to do?" I asked. "Make all the racists eat curry and get them to take lessons in tolerance?"

I walked off towards Mrs Parker-Brown's office.

Steggsy's mate, Cutler, was sitting on one of the chairs outside the principal's office when I got there.

"Don't hit me," he said, moving away in his chair.

"Don't worry about it – I'm not hitting anyone."

"You getting suspended too?" I asked him.

"Yeah – someone grassed me up."

"Same here – I thought it was you."

He looked at me and shook his head.

"I think it was Chas."

"Oh."

"So, what's your problem?" I asked, wanting to know what I had done to make him hate me.

"What problem?" he asked.

"All that racist stuff – what have I ever done to you?"

"Don't like your lot," he said, shrugging and watching me. I moved forward and he drew back.

"My *lot*?" I asked.

"Immigrants and that. You see 'em all in the paper and on the telly – takin' over they are."

"I'm not an immigrant," I told him, and for a moment I thought he was going to do that whole 'well you're OK then' thing. He didn't.

"Well you ain't English, are yer?"

I sat back in my chair and sighed.

"Where were you born, Cutler?" I asked him.

"In Mansfield – why, what's that gotta do with the ...?"

"In England, then?" I asked.

"Yeah," said Cutler.

"Well, I was born in Leicester – that's in England, too."

"I ain't thick," he said.

"You must be, because I'm as English as you."

"Nah, you ain't. You're a Paki."

"No, Cutler – even my parents ain't from Pakistan – they're from India and I'm from England."

"See?" he said. "Your mum and dad are immigrants and anyway Leicester's full of 'em – me dad says so."

"And he knows everything, does he?"

"I don't care," he said, after a while. "You lot ain't English like I'm English. This is my country."

"And it's my country, too. What are you – stupid?" I shouted. "I watch the same football as you, I support England when they play. I eat chips and that ... that's all English, innit?"

"My dad says that England was a great country before all the wogs come over," said Cutler.

But the thing was, I knew that Cutler would never change. There would always be someone to call an outsider – an Asian or an asylum seeker or the fat kid that no-one was friends with. I shook my head.

"Just get one thing into your thick head, Cutler – if you ever call me a 'Paki' again or any other racist name – I'm gonna do you like I did Steggsy ..."

Just as I was leaning over him, the door to Mrs Parker-Brown's office opened and she came out.

"GET IN HERE, SANGHA!" she shouted at me.

I looked at Cutler and smiled.

"I'll catch up with you in a bit," I said.

Cutler got all brave again. He sneered at me.

"We'll get to you first," he said, before Mrs Parker-Brown told him to shut up and marched me into her office.

She told me everything that Kitson had already said and then gave me a letter for my dad.

"Are we done?" I asked.

"If you are asking if you may go home – the answer is yes."

I stood up from my chair and picked up my bag.

"I have to say that your start here has not been a good one," said Mrs Parker-Brown, as I made my way to the door.

I turned and gave her a sarcastic smile.

"And I've been made to feel *so* welcome and all," I said, before walking out.

Chapter 8

Bad News

I had to wait ages for a bus and when I got in my dad went *mad*, calling me stupid and telling me that I was letting the racists win.

"What have you gained?" he shouted at me in Punjabi.

"It's not my fault," I replied, wishing that he'd just let me go to my room.

"Suspended from school, again. How is that helping you?"

"What was I supposed to do – just let him carry on?"

"You need to use your brain, *beteh*. Not your fists."

I started to walk away but my dad called me back, telling me that as I was not going to be in school I might as well help in the newsagent's. That it would give me something to do as I thought about the mess I had got myself into. I nearly swore.

"The mess *you've* got me into," I said, kicking a pile of local papers.

My dad gave me a death stare and then told me he was going to have a cup of tea. I picked up the papers and sat down behind the counter.

For the rest of the day I handed over fags and gave out change, trying not to get wound up. I wondered what would happen at the governors' meeting the following week. A couple of dodgy-looking men came in during the afternoon, with skinheads and tattoos, but apart from that it was quiet. Only three people made racist comments. A good day.

Around five my dad returned, telling me to go and help my mum but I wasn't in the mood. Instead I rang Jemma and told her what had happened. She already knew, asking if I was all right. I told her I was fine.

"I'm at Katie's with her and Sam," she told me. "Come over."

"Yeah, all right. I'll be ten minutes."

I went into the shop and told my dad that I was going out.

"Out? Where out?" he asked, in English.

"To see one of the few friends I've actually got."

"No," he replied, flatly.

"I'm *going*," I insisted.

"*Jaspal* ..."

In the time it took him to say my name, rage took hold and I went mad.

"I'm goin' out and I don't care what you say!"

"And I said ..."

"Stuff what you said," I told him. "If it weren't for you I wouldn't be in this hellhole or suspended from school. You think I care what *you* want anymore?"

My dad looked shocked.

"Mum's a mess. The shop gets attacked everyday. I can't walk home without getting beaten up or threatened and it's all because you didn't think about what Mum and me wanted!"

"You mind your ..." he began to say.

"GET LOST!" I shouted, storming out of the door.

I thought that he'd come out after me, shout at me in the street, but he didn't. So I walked over to Katie's house in record time, my head ready to explode.

Over and over, in my head, I was blaming him. Not the stupid racists who had made our lives a misery but my old man. A man whose only fault had been to believe the rubbish about England being a tolerant place where racism was dead. I know I was wrong to think that way but at the time it was all I *could* think about. Stupid old man – bringing us here – just to get spat at and abused ...

I calmed down at Katie's as we sat listening to CDs and I explained to her, Jemma and Sam what had happened with Steggsy and why I had been suspended from school for a week. I thought that Jemma would get mad with me, after all I had beaten up her stepbrother, but she didn't. Her biggest problem was with me not telling anyone about the racial abuse.

"How can anyone help when you don't talk about it?" she said.

"Help how?" I asked.

"Kitson would have backed you up," added Sam. "He's all right, is Kitson."

"You don't get it – none of you do. This isn't just about Steggsy and Cutler and them – it happens to my mum and dad too. Every day someone says something."

"What about the police?" asked Katie.

"They know – we've got a number for their hate-crimes officer but even that don't help. They came round once. Two hours later someone put dog shit through the letterbox."

"That's horrible," gasped Jemma.

"Horrible ain't the word, Jemma. And then there's the thugs that come into the shop every now and then. They belong to the Brotherhood of the White Fist."

"I've seen them around," admitted Sam. "They put leaflets round our estate all the time. 'Rights for Whites', immigration – that kind of thing."

"Only it ain't just them, is it?" I sighed. "They're like the extreme end of things. But there's the everyday stuff about fitting in and being properly English and that. I mean – how can I *be* any more English – I was *born* here."

"It's just ignorance," replied Katie. "We're not all like that."

"I know that, Katie, but when you get it from everywhere, every day, it's hard to think straight. I end up hating white people and that can't be right. But then some old lady calls us 'darkies' or some eleven-year-old shouts, 'Asylum seekers out!' at us and I get angry."

"I never realised it went so deep," admitted Jemma.

"You've seen the looks that we get when we're together, Jemma. Even the so-called 'liberals' don't really like it. It drives me mad – the abuse, all the lies in the papers about immigrants taking over – and it's all lies – only loads of ordinary people believe it 'cos they can't be bothered to find out the truth."

I was on a roll by that point and making myself angrier, so I tried to change the subject but it didn't work. Jemma wanted to know how I felt and Katie wanted to phone the local paper. And then Sam told us about his estate, where the people he knew didn't even know that they *were* racist.

"You'll just hear it in passing – like they're on about the weather and that. People in the supermarket or down the pub."

"That's exactly what I'm on about," I said. "How do you change that? I end up wishing I was back in Leicester where there are so many more people like me. And that can't be right either – I don't wanna have to stay in places where only other brown people live."

"Do you think that's why so many Asians live next to each other?" asked Jemma.

"Yeah – and can you blame them? Look at what's happening to my family."

The discussion went on like that for ages and by the time I looked at my watch it was gone eight in the evening. I stood up and said that I had to get home. I pulled out my mobile. The message light was flashing furiously.

"Better listen to this message," I said, as the doorbell went downstairs.

I dialled up my voice mail service as Katie went to see who was calling round. I'd no time to get to hear my message before I heard Katie cry out, "OH MY GOD!" I don't know why but I just knew that it was something to do with my mum and dad. I just *knew*.

I put my phone away and ran downstairs with Jemma. Sam was in the hallway with Chas, one of Steggsy's crew, the one that had grassed us all up, and Katie's parents.

I grabbed Chas.

"What's going on?" I shouted, right in his face, but all he did was mumble that he was 'sorry'. The next thing I knew I had my hands around his throat and I was strangling him. Katie's dad grabbed hold of my hands and prised them off as Sam spoke.

"You'd better get back to the shop – there's police and fire engines outside," he said quickly. Chas mumbled again and started to cry.

My heart sank.

Katie's parents grabbed their coats.

As we all rushed out of the house, the only thing that I could hear was Chas whimpering that he was sorry, over and over in my brain.

Chapter 9
The Final Blow

There wasn't much of my dad's shop left, nor the flat above it. It was a burnt-out, smoking ruin. It looked like it had been hit by a bomb. Police cars were parked at each end of the road and three fire engines sat outside the shop. Some of the firemen were still hosing the place down as others searched among the rubble and talked to each other.

The ambulance was 30 yards from where I stood, across the road, outside Mrs Filbert's shop. I looked for my parents but couldn't see them. Crowds were gathered at each end of the police cordon, and I saw Mr Wright at the front, to the left, talking to a policeman. I ran over to him.

"Where's my mum and dad?" I shouted, shoving past some of the onlookers.

Mr Wright saw me and pointed me out to the policeman who helped me through and asked me my name. I ignored him and looked at Mr Wright.

"Where are they?" I repeated, my head swimming and my mouth dry.

"They're in the ambulance, son," Mr Wright replied, unable to look me in the face.

I ran over to the ambulance. Two more policemen tried to hold me back. In the distance I saw the flash of camera bulbs. A policewoman came over to me. Her face was ashen. She took me to one side and told me that my dad was in the ambulance receiving treatment for burns. He had inhaled smoke and couldn't breathe properly. She asked if I was OK but I didn't reply. I wanted to see my parents. I wanted to know why she hadn't mentioned my mum. She took me to the ambulance and I got in.

My dad was lying on a trolley, with an oxygen mask on. His face and hands were a mess. Red and black with huge blisters – he didn't even look like my dad. I started to cry – tears of anger and shame and hurt. How could I not have been there when it all happened?

I turned to the policewoman.

"Where's my mum?" I whispered through my tears, knowing what she was going to say. My body went cold.

She gave me a blank look and then shook her head.

"I'm sorry, sir."

I don't know what else she said in the next five minutes because I didn't hear anything. I just went blank, pins and needles running up and down my body. I stepped out of the ambulance and walked over to the kerb. I doubled over and threw up. Over and over. I felt someone put a coat round me and turned to see Katie's dad standing beside me. I stood up slowly.

"Jas – I think you should ..."

That's when I heard Jemma scream and looked up to see her being held by Sam and Katie.

I went over to them.

"What is it?" I demanded.

"Your neighbour just told us that they pulled out two bodies ..."

"Who was the second person?" I asked, without any emotion.

"Jason," Sam told me.

"Steggsy!" I said.

"Yes," said Katie.

But I hadn't asked a question. I had just said 'Steggsy'. He must have set fire to the shop.

I felt nothing. Nothing at all. It was as though someone had taken all my emotions away and locked them up. I looked at Jemma but I just couldn't say anything. At that point I didn't care that Steggsy had died too. I might as well have been watching a television show.

Instead, I turned and walked slowly back to the ambulance which held my dad. The policewoman asked me if I had relatives that I could call. I told her that I would call an uncle on the way to the hospital and climbed into the back of the ambulance. As the doors shut I took one last look at the village ...

Become a Consultant!

Would you like to give us feedback on our titles before they are published? Contact us at the e-mail address or website below – we'd love to hear from you!

Have you read ...
Dream on
by Bali Rai

ISBN 1-842990-45-4

"If you dream it must be for real ..."

Baljit's mates knew what was what. If you were good at football, really good, you could go places. But all his old man ever talked about was duty to the family and paying bills. Baljit couldn't just go on working in his old man's chippie. He wanted out!

You can order *Dream On* directly from our website at: www.barringtonstoke.co.uk

Visit Bali Rai's website at: www.balirai.com

More Teen Titles!

Joe's Story by Rachel Anderson 1-902260-70-8
Playing Against the Odds by Bernard Ashley 1-902260-69-4
Harpies by David Belbin 1-842990-31-4
Firebug by Eric Brown 1-842991-03-5
TWOCKING by Eric Brown 1-842990-42-X
To Be A Millionaire by Yvonne Coppard 1-902260-58-9
All We Know of Heaven by Peter Crowther 1-842990-32-2
Walking with Rainbows by Isla Dewar 1-842991-30-2
The Ring of Truth by Alan Durant 1-842990-33-0
Falling Awake by Viv French 1-902260-54-6
The Wedding Present by Adèle Geras 1-902260-77-5
The Cold Heart of Summer by Alan Gibbons 1-842990-80-2
Before Night Falls by Keith Gray 1-842991-24-8
The Shadow on the Stairs by Ann Halam 1-902260-57-0
Alien Deeps by Douglas Hill 1-902260-55-4
Partners in Crime by Nigel Hinton 1-842991-02-7
The New Girl by Mary Hooper 1-842991-01-9
Dade County's Big Summer by Lesley Howarth 1-842990-43-8
Runaway Teacher by Pete Johnson 1-902260-59-7
No Stone Unturned by Brian Keaney 1-842990-34-9
The House of Lazarus by James Lovegrove 1-842991-25-6
Wings by James Lovegrove 1-842990-11-X
A Kind of Magic by Catherine MacPhail 1-842990-10-1
Stalker by Anthony Masters 1-842990-81-0
Clone Zone by Jonathan Meres 1-842990-09-8
The Dogs by Mark Morris 1-902260-76-7
Turnaround by Alison Prince 1-842990-44-6
Dream On by Bali Rai 1-842990-45-4
All Change by Rosie Rushton 1-902260-75-9
Fall Out by Rosie Rushton 1-842990-74-8
The Blessed and The Damned by Sara Sheridan 1-842990-08-X
Double Vision by Norman Silver 1-842991-00-0